Dark Deeds
at Deathwood

Good spellers please note: these letters have been reproduced exactly as written

Dark Deeds at Deathwood

Hazel Townson

Andersen Press • London

First published in 2006 by
Andersen Press Limited,
20 Vauxhall Bridge Road, London SW1V 2SA
www.andersenpress.co.uk

© 2006 Hazel Townson

British Library Cataloguing in Publication Data available

ISBN-10: 1 84270 486 9
ISBN-13: 978 1 84270 486 8

Phototypeset by Intype Libra Ltd
Printed and bound in Great Britain by
Bookmarque Ltd., Croydon, Surrey

Batch the First

24A Buckingham Buildings,
Thrumpton
15th Apr.

Dear Damian Drake,
    I hope you don't mind me writing to
you, but I saw your photo in the paper
when you were rescude from that horable
kidnaper. (Fancy him being a postman,
it makes you think!)
    I have never written to a famose
person before. My brother Steve bets you
wont write back to me but I told him you
would so don't let me down.
                    All the best from
                    Tracey Fallows

DEATHWOOD HALL
Walsea

16th Apr.

Dear Tracey,

I'm too big-hearted not to reply to your letter but I don't want you to show it to your brother Steve, just tell him I wrote and show him the envelope. I have had trouble with brothers before.

I quite enjoyed being kidnaped, I got lots of letters from girls, some wanting buttons off my shirt and stuff, but one of them actually proposed to me! Our au pair found out and told our cook Mrs Harris who told my mother, she went ballistic. But if your going to keep

writing to me you must realise I'm
not up to that sort of thing, just a
nice easy friendship.

Well, we'd better introduce
ourselves as there's nobody to do it
for us the proper way. I am a pupil
at St Aidan's Academy and quite
brainy (exept for maths and
science). I am in the soccer second
eleven (in goal), are you the sporty
type? I have no brothers and sisters
so have to rely on our French au
pair Aimee for company. She is new,
we had one called Francine but my
mother just sacked her for plucking
her eyebrows over the kitchen table.
Aimee's English is poor so she is
hopeless at Scrabble which is my
favourite game so I tried to teach
her Monopoly but she can only

think in euros. I have been a hero
before, as I rescued my dog Victor
from a well. I enclose a photo of our
house with Victor sitting on the
steps. It has 19 rooms and a
conservatory.

If you are going to keep writing
though, you'd better get a
dictionary as your spelling is awful.
Better still, why don't you e-mail me
instead of writing letters? My e-mail
address is on the back of the photo.
Don't you think 'damdeath' sounds
cool?

Get back to me soon, one way or
another.

Your new friend Damian

24A Buckingham Buildings,
Thrumpton
18th Apr.

Dear Damian,
   I was really chuffed to get your letter
on the posh notepaper with the photo of
your even posher house. It said in the
Sun that your dad is some big noise in
parliment so I guess its his notepaper
really. Your dog Victor looks okay but I
don't really like dogs, they can be fearse
and usually smell something awful.
   You must be joking about e-mails, I
haven't a computer, my mum says they
are the work of the devil and if she saw a
name like damdeath she'd have a fit. I
don't get a chance to use the school
computer for private stuff either, so it
will have to be boring old letters I'm

afraid. So get hold of some more of that posh notepaper. I have borowed a dictionary from the library, it was reference only but I snook it out and you will soon see a big improvement in my spelling.

There are 3 of us in our family, Steve, my mum and me. My dad lives in Bootle which is way up north, he got kicked out ages ago. My mum calls herself Max, she's called Maisie really but pretends Max is short for Maxine and sounds more macho anyway. That's because she and her mate Bert (i.e., Bertha) belong to this anti-everything lot called Redpeace, they're always marching about with banners saying stuff like 'make piece not war'. Mum's anti-mobiles as well so I can't ring you. She says they ruin your hearing and texting will be the death of

the English langwidge. When she found
out they were going to put a mobile mast
up at the end of our street she organised
a protest and hit a cop over the head
with her banner so she finished up in
jail overnight and had to use all our gas
and electric money as a fine. We had
candles and no hot water for yonks.

   She's a wicked speller though, you
should see some of her banners. She
makes them out of Tesco cardboard boxes,
most of our bed sheets and the posts out
of our back fence. Last week she stuck a
banner on top of the sennataf and hung
out there throwing dog-eared poppies
from last November at folks passing by.
That banner said 'fight for a peaceful
future for our kids' but this kid (me)
finished up peacefully sorting out two
days of washing up left rotting in the

*sink, going to the laundret, fetching the
dinner from the chippie and ironing our
Steves black shirt, he's in a group called
the Dropouts. I did show him your letter,
he wouldn't have believed me if I hadn't,
but don't worry, he's not much interested
in me now he's going steddy with this
snooty cow Belinda. She's horable, she
treats me like a slave. She tried to send
me to the shops for her ciggies but I said
I'm too young, go and nick your own.
She's a hairdresser at Lovelilocks, I've
seen her in the sallon doing comb-ups
with a ciggie stuck in her mouth, it's a
wonder she hasn't set somebodys perm on
fire.*

   *My only two sports are boxing
(watching the box!) and sprinting (from
trouble). Our Steve says I'm the best
sprinter for miles around and have worn*

the boots off several cops. I think
football's pretty boring and being in goal
sounds like the most boring bit of all.

What do your folks get up to? Id love
to know how the other half lives so write
soon and tell me.

Your intrested friend,
Tracey

P.S. Why can't that show-off Aimee spell
her name AMY like everybody else?

DEATHWOOD HALL
Walsea

20th Apr.

Dear Tracey,

Thanks for your letter. Your mum sounds like most of my dad's politicle friends who are always laying down the law but don't really know what they are on about. I like the sound of the Dropouts though. Does Steve play the guitar? I've always fancied doing that but my mother makes me have violin lessons which I hate. I sound like a strangled cat.

You probably don't like dogs because you have only come across mongrels, not good pedigree stock like Victor. The only thing he smells of is Klassi-champ shampoo, he gets bathed in it every day, it is six quid a bottle.

My folks don't get up to anything much. My dad snoozes on the benches in parliament when it's in session which is almost never, and my mother tells Mrs Harris what to cook for dinner when we are having gests, which is nearly every day. Aimee is supposed to look after me and keep me out of the way when the gests are here but I usually snoop about a bit, you'd be amazed what goes on.

It's a very lonely life though so I was wondering if you'd like to come over and meet me sometime. It would have to be a very cloak and dagger affair as I am not supposed to go out on my own. It can be done though, especially when Aimee is busy being chatted up by our assistant gardener Ricky. I sometimes meet my friend Frankie, she is good at cloak and dagger, her surname is Bond like 007, but she is stuck at her aunt's at present and can't always get away. So what do you say? How are you fixed for transport?

Your pining friend,
Damian

P.S. Aimee is French as I already told you and that's how they spell Amy in France.

24A Buckingham Buildings,
Thrumpton
21st Apr.

Dear Damian,
    Yeah, meeting you would be cool, but I
suppose I'll have to be the one to make
the effort and come to you since you keep
dropping down wells and getting
kidnapped. But it will have to be by bike
as I wouldn't be seen dead on a bus and
my mum thinks cars are polluters of the
earth and the ruin of good maners and
have made everybody into lazy road
ragers, especially four wheel drives, and
we couldn't afford one anyway. But I am
a good biker, its healthy and great for
getting your legs in shape. I just need a
map but I am working on it. Actally
Steve has a map in case the Dropouts

ever get on the road (some hopes!) but he won't lend it to me, he says I wont be able to follow it, never mind folding it proply, the sexist pig. But if I go biking any distance mum always makes Steve go with me in case I get mugged, so he could read his own map and show me the way. I'd have to bribe him with my paper-round dosh but it would be worth it, what do you think?

Steve doesn't play the guitar, he is the Dropouts lead singer which is worse than your violin, he has a voice like a half-murdered magpie.

Raring to go,
Tracey

DEATHWOOD HALL
Walsea

23rd Apr.

Dear Tracey,

Well, I would have liked to meet
you, I like your sense of humour,
but I'm sorry, I couldn't let you
bring Steve. He must never come
here, I told you what I thought
about brothers. If you knew what
trouble Frankie's brother had
caused us you wouldn't have
suggested it. I'm a bit miffed
actually. First you show him my
letter when I specially asked you not
to, then you want to bring him here!
Well, I think we'd better call a halt
at that before its too late. Sorry, but

you have to understand what it's like
for me here, being watched and
checked up on all the time, and still
looking over my shoulder
wondering when the next villain will
come creeping up.

Your might-have-been friend,

Damian

24A Buckingham Buildings,
Thrumpton
26th Apr.

Dear Damian,

So how do you know I'm not a villain,
then? It's okay, I'm not, so you should
just calm down hothead, you've got it all
wrong, and anyway you should never let
brothers scare you off, most of them are
pussycats.

Anyway, Steve wouldn't be hanging
out with us, there'll be plenty of things
for him to do in a seaside place like
Walsea. E.g., he could play the fruit
machines on the pier – (with MY paper-
round money!) – he'd like that, he has a
gambler's nose. He'll just drop me off,
then collect me again after. Anyway he'll
be a let-out if mum finds out I've come.

She doesn't like me going off too far on my own, she says you never know what might happen, the roads of Britain are gutters of inikwity. Luckily she spotted the photo of your house and thought it looked pretty smart, well worth a visit, so I'll remind her of that if she gets too stroppy.

Your Frankie's brother sounds a right moron, we behave better than that in Thrumpton. I don't know why you keep up with her if she causes you nothing but trouble. So why don't you ditch her before I come? Because YES I am still coming to see you. You've invited me now and it's rude to go back on it. So even if I have a postcard from you telling me not to, I'll come nocking on those fancy gates of yours at about 3 o'clock

next Saturday afternoon, just let
anybody try and stop me!
       Your determined friend,
       Tracey

DEATHWOOD HALL
Walsea

28th Apr.

Dear Tracey,

All right, you win, seeing I'm desperate for a bit of company, but please note I am NOT SCARED of anybody, I'm a double hero, remember, and actually playing in goal is pretty tough. But you MUST NOT come knocking at our gates or show up anywhere near the house as you will get me into terrible trouble. I'll meet you at the front of the pier, near the turnstile where you pay to go on. I'll be tossing some yellow ping pong balls in my hands so you will recognise me. I look forward to seeing you but your Steve had better disappear fast, otherwise our first meeting could also be our last, it's up to you.

In haste,

Your equally determined friend,

Damian

Batch the Second

DEATHWOOD HALL
Walsea

1st May

Dear Tracey,

I hope you got home okay. Did Steve collect you as promised, or did his nose get stuck to the fruit-machines? Anyway, I enjoyed our date, it was wicked, despite having to trundle your bike up and down the prom.

So you're a redhead? You never said. Frankie says all redheads have terrible tempers and you did smoulder a bit when I said it was time to go. But you have a good sense of humour and we had some rare old laughs so even before you left I was already planning for you to come to Walsea again. At least I was until I got home and ran right into trouble.

It turns out Aimee rumbled us. I told her I was going to bed with a migrane and didn't want to be disturbed, but she heard me sneak out and followed me. She hid behind the deck chair keeosk and saw us meeting, and now she is holding it over me, threatening to tell Mrs Harris if I try it again (or maybe even if I don't!). Then Mrs H. would tell my mother who would stop me going out (except for school) ever again. I'd be like the prisoner of Zenda. So we have to shut Aimee up somehow. Any ideas (short of murder!)?

Write back as soon as you get this.

Your worried friend,

Damian

3, Heaven Street,
Thrumpton
2nd May

Dear Max,

Fred says you're not coming with us on this anti-dog-fouling demo next Saturday. Going to a party, I hear! Well, it's all right for some, but you don't get away with it altogether. We still need more banners off you. Fetch them round to ours no later than Friday night. If I'm not in, leave them in the yard.

Fred suggested DOGGY DO'S TURN STREETS TO LOOS but I reckon that's too tame. We need something sharper, such as DOGS WHO DO SHOULD DIE! Anyway, I'm sure you'll come up trumps as usual.

By the way, I saw your Steve

canoodling in the park with that tarty blonde from the hairdresser's. You want to watch her, she has a temper like a scalded rottweiler when she's roused. She once went for Mrs Hackett with the trimming scissors.

Enjoy the party!

Cheers,
Bert

24A, Buckingham Buildings,
Thrumpton
2nd May

Dear Damian,
I'm writing back straight away like
you said, but I nearly didn't, I was hurt.
Fancy discussing me with that bighead
Frankie! As a matter of fact redheads are
twice as brainy as brunets and three
times as brainy as blondes so tell her to
put that in her book of noledge. And I
thought you said she was away at her
auntie's?
Anyway, it turns out your Aimee
wasn't the only spy, our Steve spotted
HER dodging about behind that keeosk
and fancied what he saw. He keeps
wondering who she was and yammering
on about her and how fit and trendy she

looked. So why don't you tell Aimee she
has an admierer and offer to fix a
meeting with him as long as she keeps
quiet about us? Tell her he is the lead
singer in a band, it will impress her and
I enclose a photo he had took for the gigs.
It's tarted up and flatters him like mad
but it will probably do the trick. If it
does, I could fix it all at this end for
next Saturday, it would be good to get
one over on that snooty cow Belinda.
But I have my price. You will have to
take me to that posh new Macdonalds on
the prom next time I come. It smelt great
when we walked past it and made my
mouth water.

My mum wont let us go to
Macdonalds or Burgerking or any of
that lot, she says they are at the bottom of
the worlds obeesity problem and should

all be bulldozed and made into a
massive giant barbekew. So is it a date?

My dad turned up today, mega
surprise! He lives in Bootle which is the
back of beyond and I hardly ever see him.
He called to ask if he could take me to
the zoo next Saturday but mum wouldn't
let him. She says zoos are wicked cruel
places and should all be shut down. If
she had her way all the keepers would be
put behind bars and fed raw meat
driping with blood. I was mad because I
wanted to go, I've never been to a zoo
and anyway I want to get to know my
dad, I might even like him. So that's why
I want to fix this meeting for Saturday to
stop me moping about feeling sorry for
myself. I wouldn't even have my mum to
entertain me with her anti-goings-on,
she'll be away all day and maybe

overnight. She says she'll be helping out at some posh party. (She does this sometimes, she calls it in-fill-traitoring which is posh talk for brainwashing everyone she gets near enough to chat up. She usually homes in on the bigwigs like vicars and mayors, hoping she can get them to change the world.)

So I'm planning to come with Steve, then, and you can make up for the treat I've missed by standing me a good nosh-up at Macdonalds.

Your half-orphan friend,
Tracey the fixer

DEATHWOOD HALL
Walsea

4th May

Dear Fixer,

Well done, you are a red-headed genius after all! I think pairing off Aimee with Steve is a great idea, so sure I'll stand you a good feed at Macdonald's if you can fix it up. I'm not proud and could do with sinking my teeth into some good, solid food instead of this holesome rubbish we get here which is no good for filling you up. I've already got Aimee interested, she seemed to like the photo and is raring to youmiliate moon-eyed Ricky and stop him pestering her, he always

has black fingernails and is beneath
her notice. (He's our gardener's
assistant, who fancies her like mad
and keeps giving her roses he's
nicked off our bushes). So lets strike
while the iron is hot.

You have picked a good day as
well, because next Saturday will be
chaos here as the Home Secretary is
coming to dinner as well as some
miner royal and all the staff will be
running around like headless
chickens, not to mention my parents
and all the extras brought in for the
day. Aimee is supposed to keep me
well out of the way at times like this,
so we should be able to make a
smart getaway under cover of the
general panic.

We will meet you and Steve at the

same place as before, but this time I won't need the ping pong balls.

Your now familiar friend,

Damian

24A, Buckingham Buildings,
Thrumpton
5th May

Dear Bert,
 3 new banners as requested. Hope
the doggy demo goes well. No need to
be jealous about Saturday as I'll be
working even harder than you. Lots of
highly influential folks to chat up.
Also I might even get some new
recruits from the lower orders.
 Up the Anti's!
                    Cheers,
                    Max

24A, Buckingham Buildings,
Thrumpton
5th May

Dear Damian

I filled Steve in about our plans and he played it cool. He says lots of girls fancy him, but he doesn't mind giving this one a go. I know he's never took out a French chick before, it will up his street cred and I saw the gleam in his eye. So I know he will come, no probs.

What do you think they'll do? Back row of the pictures or a ride in the tunnel of love? Maybe we could go to the pictures as well as Macdonalds. It's my one chance, Mum won't let us near a cinema, she says they are hotbeds of violence, nightmares and putting silly ideas into kids' heads. She's never been

to a film in her life but she picketed the
Odeon when they were showing Silence of
the Lambs because our next door neibour
Mrs Gubbins fainted half way through
it. The manager came out and told mum
she'd got it all wrong, it was just a love
story about a deaf shepherd boy and told
her to go home but she told him he was a
rotten liar and smashed a hole in the
ticket window.

    See you on Sat then, I can't wait. Pity
about the ping pong balls, you could
have put your cap on the floor and
pretended you were an unemploid juggler.
                Your genius friend,
                    Tracey

P.S. I didn't know royals went down the
pit.

Batch the Third

DEATHWOOD HALL
Walsea

7th May

Dear Tracey,

   Well, I hope you enjoyed today, especially the burgers and fries, not to mention the four doughnuts, it cost me two weeks' spends. I don't know how you could eat all that, you are as bad as Frankie, she eats like a horse. But I think we will give Mac's a miss next time, as I have a bit of a stummach upset and am writing this on a stool in my bathroom.

   Still, it did the trick, we now have Aimee in our power. She keeps wittering on about Steve all the time, she is really smitten (yuk!).

But if she tells on me now she knows I'll tell on her. Not only would she be in trouble for letting me escape, but I found out that she had sneaked Steve into her room which is forbidden, especially when folk like miner royals are coming to dinner. So we can now go ahead with any future plans.

You wouldn't believe the fuss here about this dinner party with the Home Sec. and everybody. All that booze, nosh and fancy silver, plus private detectives and extra girls waiting on. If that much energy went into running the country and espeshially the trains and buses the world would be a much better place.

Looking forward to seeing you

lots more, and to feeling better
soon,

                Cheers,
                Damian

P.S. Royals don't go down the pit as
you very well know. Miner just
means they are not as important as
the Queen.

24A, Buckingham Billet,
Thrumpton
9th May

Dear Damian,

Sorry about your STOMACH upset —
(note that spelling, you're the one who
needs a dictionary!). You will have to eat
more junk food and toughen up your
insides.

I expect by now you will have seen on
the telly news how my dad climbed
Walsea tower last Sat. in his Gandalf
outfit with one of mum's banners he'd
nicked. It said ANIMALS ARE
IMPORTANT TOO but he blocked out
the ANIMALS and put DADS instead.
He'd found out I'd gone to Walsea and
came to wisk me off to the zoo after all,
but he couldn't find me so this was his

Plan B. He was perched on a giddy ledge yelling 'Where are you Tracey I can hardly remember what you look like!'. Seems it was six hours before the police talked him down. I'm glad I missed it, it was bad enough seeing it on the news, knowing all my friends would be watching. I was so glued to it that I almost missed seeing that cow Belinda sneaking up behind me and putting something in my bag. She hates me so much for not being her slave that it could have been a bomb for all I knew, or at least a nasty firework. But when I looked I couldn't find anything there except the usual junk, one nearly empty purse, doorkey, screwed up tisues, extra-strong nail-file for stabbing muggers, lippy and your latest letters, so I guess she must have borowed my lippy, the

sneaky mare. Ugh! I scraped the top lair
off it just in case.

How about another meeting soon?
Steve can't make it next Sat as he has a
wedding gig in some village called
Pockmark or something. It's very last
minute, they only get gigs when somebody
else has cried off. But I know the way
now, I don't need him any more so I
could come on my own. How about it?

Champing at the bit,

Tracey

10th May

Dear Tracey,

Sorry, but I can't see you next Sat as we are in termoil here. When the Home Secretary got back from dining at ours last Saturday he found out all his secret papers had gone missing from his briefcase that he left in our upstairs gest dressing room, and it has turned into a major panic. By Monday we had MI5 here searching everywhere, even Victor's kennel and the rakings from the Aga, and on top of all that AIMEE HAS DISAPPEARED, though we didn't notice right away as Sunday was her day off. (Her room is right next door to the gest dressing room where the papers were, is that significant or what??)

My mother is frantic, she says it was a big responsibility, not to mention a mistake, the Home Sec. coming straight from some important meeting and having to bring secret papers with him to a dinner party. Mrs Harris reckons those papers were stuff the Home Sec. daren't leave at home as they are probably dynamite. She says rumour has it he's been threatening to have all folks under 40 forced off the streets by 9 o clock at weekends, plus windfarms in every park in the land, and if stuff like that gets out it could be the ruin of my dad's career, never mind the Home Sec.'s.

Well, my mother has decided that we must have had an intruder who took Aimee hostage and went off with the papers so now she is worried I might get kidnaped again. She has told ALL the staff to keep a close eye on me (yuk!) and to make sure Victor is not far away at all times. It's a wonder they haven't chained me to the banisters! I'm garded worse than the crown jewels, you'd never get near me. So why don't you go to that Pockmark wedding instead? (I suppose you mean Pockton, it's quite a nice place, my uncle George used to live there.) You could go as the Dropouts mascot. Think of all that

free nosh and shampain, you'd have
a wicked time.

I know Aimee's a bit of a pest but
I can't help worrying about her,
even though I know from
experience that kidnapers are never
as clever as they think they are.
Write back and cheer me up.

Your miserable prisoner,
Damian

24A, Buckingham Bogs,
Thrumpton
12th May

Dear Crown Jewel (but not so
sparkling!),
  I'm not that gulable! I know you
have spun me this yarn so you can go
and see that Frankie floosie on Sat.
Well, it so happens I have a date for
Sat. with somebody who has never
stood me up with crackbrained excuses
and who isn't always moaning and
boasting about being kidnapped either.
What's more, I won't need to bike till
my legs drop off, he only lives on our
estate.

  Your ex-friend,
  Tracey Fallows

P.S. However much I now dispise you, I am still big-hearted enough to hope Aimee gets found in one piece, but I can't say I'm bothered about any secret papers.

DUMP
DEATHWOOD ~~HALL~~
Walsea

13th May

Dear Tracey,

This time it's you who've got it all wrong, I'm NOT seeing Frankie on Saturday. I was telling the truth. You must have seen it on the news that we had a burglary here, though it didn't say what of. Anyway, maybe you'll believe me when I tell you I did some secret snooping and found a few clues. Footprints in the garden for a start, and more footprints right through the conservatory where the dinner gests never went. They were smallish footprints and could have been a woman's. But the best bit was, I found a locket on a broken chain. It has STOB engraved on it and inside there's a lock of hair and a tiny photo of this poser like some third rate soap actor, he looks vagely familiar as they do, but I couldn't really place him. Maybe they can get his DNA from the lock of hair if it's his. Should I go on snooping on my own, do you think, or should I tell MI5?

I've been wondering what sort of name STOB is. Do you know any soap stars with names like that? I don't get to watch much soap, my mother says it's infra dig which is Latin for 'in for a cheap joke', usually at the governments expense. Do you reckon maybe the Home Sec. was going to shut down all soap

programmes so this actor had to
steal the papers before they got
signed? It would be a good motive if
he thought he'd finish up on the
dole after all that fame.

Your dazzling (and
dazzled) detective,
Damian

24A, Buckingham Badlands,
Thrumpton
15th May

Dear Detective Damian,

Well, all right I admit I didn't have a date for Sat either, I just wanted to make you jealous.

So you've turned detective, have you? Aren't you the clever one? A bit too clever if you ask me. That locket probably belongs to Aimee and got ripped from her neck when she was being dragged away by the kidnappers. Or how about your preshus Frankie? I bet SHE gets through your gates, no problem. So I wouldn't bother showing it to the cops if I were you, they'll only cart you off for questioning and then before you know it

you'll have confesed to all sorts of things
you never did.

    That's what just happened to my dad.
When he was up Walsea tower the cops
found out he had a Tesco carrier bag
with an alarm clock and a load of fuse
wire in it. It was only stuff he'd bought
for his flat but they've now got him down
as a suicide bomber. My mum says serve
him right, the country is littered with
folks trying to blow useless bits of it up
and the sooner the better, it will bring
everybody to there senses about real
catastrofies and make them stop claiming
compensashun for every bit of a bruise.

    I asked around about STOB though,
and my mate Mandy says she thinks
there's somebody who used to be in
Eastenders called STOBbins Or it might
be short for S. TOBias or ST.OBeron.

By the way, that cow Belinda looks a bit worse for wear all of a sudden (three cheers!) she has a black eye and scratches on her cheek. She must have had a set-to with our Steve, she gets mad when he's off with the Dropouts all the time and won't take her anywhere, but he's not usually the violent type. Anyway, lets hope that's the end of her as far as this family's concerned.

Why don't I come over and help you find more clues? With things this desperate you need some high class support.

Yours eagerly,
Tracey

DEATHWOOD ~~HALL~~ DREGS
Walsea

16th May

Dear Tracey,

Thanks for your intresting suggestions and offer of more help with the sloothing, but you are more use where you are, just using your brains and asking around, and anyway this place is garded like Fort Knocks at present so we'd never get together. But keep at it, you might just come up with another flash of genius.

My dad is very upset about these missing papers as some people are starting to think he took them, as well as sending Aimee packing

because she stuck her head round
her door and saw him do it, so he is
walking around with a face like
pickled cabbage. If those bloomin
papers don't get found soon, not to
mention Aimee alive or dead, I
think he will loop the loop.

Gotta go now, MI5's here again.
It's a good job we didn't start e-
mailing after all as they have been
nosing about on my computer.

Your hunted crony,

Damian

P.S. Frankie has just come up with a
great idea. She says STOB might be
S – TO – B which would make one
dollop of a difference. Somebody
called S could have given that locket
TO somebody called B. And now I

come to look at it under my magnifying glass there's a bit of a space beside the first and last letters, so she could be right. Good old Frankie, eh?

24A, Buckingham Bolthole,
Thrumpton
18th May

Dear Two-timer,

I thought you and me were supposed
to be sorting this crime together? Fancy
dragging that Frankie in! What does she
know about it?

Anyway, she's not that clever, I was
just going to sugest the same thing, only
being that much brighter than her I can
take it further. Because guess what, it
could stand for 'Steve TO Belinda' so I
bet our Steve was going to give that
locket to Belinda but he dropped it when
he was snogging your Aimee. It was
Belindas birthday the day before
yesterday but I know for a fact Steve
didn't give her a present (unless you

count her black eye and scratches). So that means the locket has nothing to do with your VIPs. (Good thing you didn't let on to MI5.)

Well, how's that for a bit of classy detective work? Tell that not-so-good old Frankie that she has a rip-roaring red-headed rival.

Your superier friend,
Tracey

P.S. Here's some more classy detective work. Have you thought, Aimee could just have got fed up looking after you and gone back to France, who could blame her? Folks her age are always taking off without a word, it's called a mid-life crisis. Our Steve has just done exactly the same, we think he's gone to

*our gran's to sweet-talk some cash out of
her for a new drum kit for the Dropouts.*

DROP-IN
DEATHWOOD ~~HALL~~
Walsea

20th May

Dear Tracey,

I wish you'd stop going on about Frankie. I told you she is my best friend, too bad if you don't like it. People are entitled to have more than one friend. Anyway, I think she put two and two together really well, and it doesn't prove the locket had nothing to do with the crime. Suppose it was YOUR STEVE who nicked the Home Sec.'s papers in case he was going to ban all gigs or slap a massive tax on them? You must admit it looks mighty suspicious him disappearing as well.

Yours gloomily,
Damian

2b, Crackwood Court,
Thrumpton
20th May

Dear Rotten, Miserable, Two-timing Steve,

You really are the limit! I know exactly what's been going on because I found some letters in your Tracey's bag. But somehow I don't think your bit of French ooh-la-la will be wanting to see you again. I certainly don't want to, and just to make it plain I would have sent back that cheap, nasty locket you gave me, only I've lost it.

Goodbye and good riddance!
Belinda G. Blenkinsop

Batch the Fourth

12, rue Hélène,
13100
Aix en Provence
le 11 mai

Mon Cher Steve,
    I know I have agree to ask some
leave to spend quelques jours with you
at Margate but it is ne pas so easy. I
expect you hear about that which is
going on at Deathwood, and more
worse, this femme terrible has come to
my room and pull my hair and kick
and hit me. She say I have thief you
away but I not know who she is. Now
I do not any more have such a beau
visage and am frightening to see you.
So I am deciding to go home to mes
parents. I not know if I daring to come

back but I will write you more. I
remembering avec plaisir a good fun
with you. Au revoir,

> *Votre amie,*
>
> *Aimée*

24A, Buckingham Bucket
shop,
Thrumpton
21st May

Dear Damian,
    Guess what, a letter arrived from
France today for our Steve, it took ten
days, I thought our post was bad
enough! So as Steve isn't here I steamed
it open. It was from your Aimee and it
seems Steve had fixed up a rondyvoo
with her in Margate, the sly old so-and-
so, and that's where he's sneaked off to,
but she's stood him up and gone home to
mummy, he won't half be blazing mad.
Her English isn't very good so I didn't
understand it all, but it seems she got
beaten up by some woman, probably the
one who robbed your VIP. You'd best tell

your folks where she is, then the cops can stop digging up your garden.

There was another letter for Steve from that snooty cow Belinda but I didn't even bother reading that, I just ripped it up and shoved it down the lav.

Have they found your bloke's secret papers yet? I wish they'd get a move on because I'm dying of boredom here and want to come and see you again. Give me an update.

Yours impatiently,
Tracey

DOLDRUMS

DEATHWOOD ~~HALL~~
Walsea

24th May

Dear Tracey,

I already knew about Aimee going home as my mother eventually found a number to ring for her folks in France and she had a letter as well, at the same time you did. My parents were relieved in one way, knowing A. wasn't murdered, but pretty mad in another and I got hauled over the coals because they thought I'd known Aimee's plans, which of course I hadn't. So just to sweeten everybody up a bit I showed them the locket, though I didn't mention our theory about Steve TO

Belinda. My mother has now given it
to MI5 so the whole thing is out of
our hands. Pity, as I was just starting
to enjoy the sloothing. Anyway, let's
hope things will soon calm down
and we can get together again. If
Aimee doesn't come back there will
have to be a new au pair, but don't
worry, this time I will make it clear
who's boss, right from the start.

Never say die!

Your indommitable friend,

Damian

REDPEACE H. Q.
Thrumpton.
24th May

To the Home Secretary,
Houses of Parliament,
London.

Dear Sir,

Certain papers have recently fallen into the hands of REDPEACE, a group of which I have the honour to be leader. Our aims are to fight against anything that detracts from a safe, peaceful, orderly and worthwhile existence – (such as road rage, salty beefburgers, bashed-up bus shelters knee-deep in broken glass, outrageous curfews and windfarms in every park) – and the material in these papers, which we have been studying at length, gives us great cause for alarm.

We therefore wish to point out that unless you revoke all the plans mentioned in these papers we will take over every public library in Britain and burn every written word that ever existed. Nothing will be saved, not even Magna Carta, Maeve Binchy, slimming recipes, bus timetables or Old Moore's Almanack.

Yours faithfully,

Ramona Redpeace (which is not my real name so it will be pointless to try to track me down.)

Flat 21,
Wackford Court,
Bootle
26th May

Dear Damian,

Well, so much has happened in the last 2 days that I'm stuck where to begin. My mum got arrested again, goodness knows what she's been up to now. Mrs Gubbins next door says it was MI5 who took her off this time. She reckons it's something to do with an anonnymus letter sent to somebody important in the government, but Mrs G thinks they've got the wrong woman as they kept calling her Ramona! Imagine my mum with a name like that!! And just when I need our Steve to lean on it turns out he's cleared off to France to shack up with your Aimee. He rang our gran to ask her to tell me, as we have no phone and he says neither of them will be coming back. The Dropouts have had to pawn their drumkit to pay their debts, so they've had to disband.

But you know what they say, it's a pretty black cloud that has no turning, and lo and behold my dad came to get me! He said fate had smiled on him at last, I couldn't stay at home all by myself, so here I am in his flat in Bootle. It's not bad, a bit sparse but clean and tidy and I think we'll get on okay as he likes a good laugh same as me.

Trouble is, Bootle's a heck of a long way from Walsea, too far to bike. At first I thought that was it and I'd never see you again. But then my dad told me a secret. He said when he was up Walsea

tower he sussed out an even better
publicity spot for the Dads' Campain.
He's been planning it all out and he's
borrowed a van to drive two of his mates
down to Walsea. They are chucked-out
dads as well and are going to hang a
massive banner over the Big Dipper on
Walsea Pleasureland. My dad doesn't
need to climb with them now he's got me,
but he says he can't abandon his mates
altogether.

So guess what, I've booked myself a
seat in the van and he's going to drop
me off at our usual spot in front of the
pier next Saturday. Just you be there,
ping pong balls or not.

Looking forward to seeing you again,
Love from Tracey

DEATHWOOD HALL
Walsea

26th May

Mrs Jocelyn Brimly-Fanshawe,
Domestic Staff Recruiting Agency,
High Street,
Walsea.

Dear Madam,

As you are aware, I have used your agency countless times for the recruitment of extra waitresses for special dinner parties at the Hall, and in all fairness I have to admit that I have usually been highly satisfied with the standard of staff supplied.

However, your latest offering was a complete disaster. One woman, Mrs Ramona Redpeace, actually turned out to be not only lazy and poorly trained but also a thief of highly sensitive material which almost caused a national emergency. I don't know how this woman came to be on your books, but you should remove her from them forthwith. In any case she is likely to be out of circulation for some time to come as she is presently being questioned by MI5.

I have deducted the cost of her labour from my cheque (enclosed) and will be seeking help elsewhere in the future.

Yours faithfully,
Amanda Drake

DEATHWOOD HALL
Walsea

26th May

Dear Belinda,

You will remember me, I am the gardner who patched you up after that fight you had with the stuck-up French floosy. You showed her what was what, and no mistake, she soon scurrid off back to France.

I hope your woonds are now feeling better and wonder if you would care for a night out. I could show you a realy good time, I scrub up okay and will make sure my fingernails are clean.

        Your great admyrer,

            Ricky

'Thespian Bower',
Shakespeare Terrace,
Walsea.
26th May

Dear Damian Drake,

Some time ago I spotted you juggling at the entrance to Walsea pier. It has taken me quite a time to track you down, but I am now able to write to invite you to join us at WADS (Walsea Amateur Dramatic Society).

As you probably know, we have our own little theatre just behind the gas works and an enthusiastic membership of all ages. We are currently planning a production of a musical play about a circus, written by myself, entitled 'Balls Up!', for the cast of which we urgently need a juvenile juggler.

We hope you may be interested in auditioning for this part. If so, please come along to the theatre at seven p.m. tomorrow evening.

We can guarantee you lots of fun and an ever-widening circle of friends.

Yours sincerely,
Fenella Mouldsley-Burton

Other Books by Hazel Townson